To my children and all those who believe in unicorns — AD
To my children, Clare and Max — JB

Picture Window Books are published by Capstone,
1710 Roe Crest Drive, North Mankato, Minnesota 56003
www.mycapstone.com

Text © 2017 Aleesah Darlison
Illustrations © 2017 Jill Brailsford

Library of Congress Cataloging-in-Publication Data
Cataloging-in-publication data is available on the Library of Congress website.
ISBN 978-1-4795-6550-4 (library binding)

Time is running out to find princess Aveena, heir of Haartsfeld kingdom.
Krystal and the Riders must search the fairy forest of Ingawan to find her. Once
they do, can Krystal convince her to come home and claim her thrown?

Editor: Nikki Potts
Designer: Kayla Rossow
Art Director: Juliette Peters
Production Specialist: Kathy McColley
The illustrations in this book were created by Jill Brailsford.

Cover design by Walker Books Australia Pty Ltd
Cover images: Rider, symbol, and unicorns © Gillian Brailsford 2011;
lined paper © iStockphoto.com/Imageegaml;
parchment © iStockphoto.com/Peter Zelei

The illustrations for this book were created with black pen, pencil,
and digital media.

Design Element: Shutterstock: Slanapotam

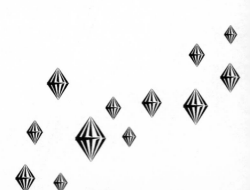

Printed and bound in China.
009959S17

UNICORN RIDERS

Krystal's Charge

Aleesah Darlison

Illustrations by
Jill Brailsford

PICTURE WINDOW BOOKS
a capstone imprint

Willow & Obecky

Willow's symbol
- a violet—represents being watchful and faithful

Uniform color
- green

Unicorn
- Obecky has a black opal horn.
- She has the gifts of healing and strength.

Ellabeth & Fayza

Ellabeth's symbol
- a hummingbird—represents energy, persistence, and loyalty

Uniform color
- red

Unicorn
- Fayza has an orange topaz horn.
- She has the gift of speed and can also light the dark with her golden magic.

Quinn & Ula

Quinn's symbol
- a butterfly—represents change and lightness

Uniform color
- blue

Unicorn
- Ula has a ruby horn.
- She has the gift of speaking with Quinn using mind-messages.
- She can also sense danger.

Krystal & Estrella

Krystal's symbol
- a diamond—represents perfection, wisdom, and beauty

Uniform color
- purple

Unicorn
- Estrella has a pearl horn.
- She has the gift of enchantment.

The
Unicorn Riders' World

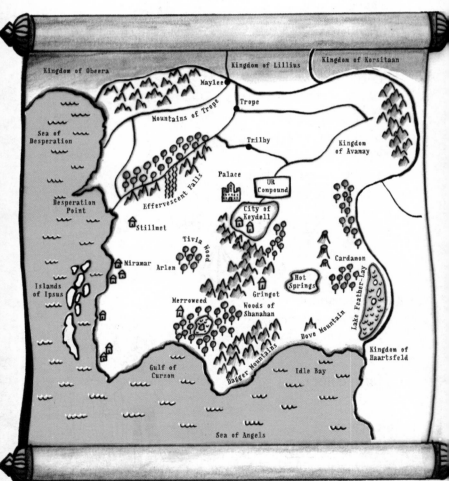

The Unicorn Riders of Avamay

Under the guidance of their leader, Jala, the Unicorn Riders and their magical unicorns protect the Kingdom of Avamay from the threats of evil Lord Valerian.

Decades ago, Lord Valerian forcefully took over the neighboring kingdom of Obeera. He began capturing every magical creature across the eight kingdoms. Luckily, King Perry saved four of Avamay's unicorns. He asked the unicorns to help protect Avamay. And that's when ordinary girls were chosen to be the first Unicorn Riders.

A Rider is chosen when her name and likeness appear in The Choosing Book, which is guarded by Jala. It holds the details of all the past, present, and future Riders. No one can see who the future Riders will be until it is time for a new Rider to be chosen. Only then will The Choosing Book display her details.

• CHAPTER 1 •

KRYSTAL HUNG UPSIDE DOWN, staring at the crowd gathered in the marquee below. All heads tilted upward. All eyes were glued to her.

What if I fall? she wondered as her heart thudded in her chest.

Still upside down, her gaze sought the other Unicorn Riders. Willow, Quinn, and Ellabeth watched her intently. Quinn's hands were clasped in front of her as if she were praying. The Riders' faithful unicorns stood nearby. Krystal's unicorn, Estrella, whinnied and tossed her mane nervously as she watched Krystal.

Krystal took a deep breath. *All right, let's do this,* she thought.

Releasing her right ankle, she stretched her leg out so that she dangled by her foot, which was wrapped around the trapeze. The narrow bar was held in place by two long ropes attached to the marquee ceiling. Below, there was no net to catch Krystal if she fell. She'd insisted on performing without it, claiming her act would be more dramatic that way. Now she wasn't sure her decision had been wise.

Remember your routine, she told herself. *You've practiced this hundreds of times.*

Twirling around and around the bar, Krystal performed spins and turns that made the crowd gasp. Her act was one of many to be performed during Princess Serafina's birthday festivities, and she was determined to stand out.

Krystal's confidence grew rapidly. But on the last movement, she misjudged her turn. Her fingers slipped and she lost hold of the bar and toppled down. Somehow, she managed to grip on with her knee. It was all that saved her from falling. For several frightening moments, Krystal dangled awkwardly, like a rag doll.

Down below, the crowd thought it was all part of her act.

Krystal reached up with shaking hands and grasped the bar. She sat upright, took a second to steady herself, then held her arms wide for the applause. When the crowd began cheering, she reached for the rope and swung over to the ladder before sliding all the way down and landing on Estrella's back.

"Go on, girl," Krystal told Estrella. Her hands still trembled, though she tried to hide it. "No one will mind if you use your enchantment magic. It will make us both look better."

Estrella reared up and sent a flurry of magical sparks into the air. The crowd was delighted with her radiant beauty. People cheered and gave them a standing ovation. Krystal grinned with relief.

Princess Serafina strode over to offer Krystal a bouquet of blood-red roses.

"Thank you, Princess Serafina," Krystal said. "But shouldn't you be the one receiving flowers today? After all, it's your birthday."

"Not this time," Serafina said, smiling. "These are for you. I couldn't have asked for a better birthday gift than your performance, Krystal. That last stunt was death defying."

Krystal blushed, but didn't say anything. She didn't want Serafina knowing she'd made a near fatal error.

"It was death defying," Queen Heart said as she strolled over with Jala, the Unicorn Riders' leader. "We'd better be careful, Jala. Krystal might run away to join the circus."

Jala laughed. "I hope not," she said. "We need Krystal to help protect Avamay."

It was the Unicorn Riders' job to protect their queen and their people from danger and evil forces.

"I'd never join the circus," she declared proudly. "Not while I'm a Unicorn Rider."

"You'd better not," Ellabeth said. "We'd miss you."

"You were brilliant, Krystal!" Quinn beamed.

"You made it seem so effortless," said Willow.

"That's the skill of a great trapeze artist," Jala said. "Making difficult moves look easy. However, I can certainly testify to the many hours Krystal spent perfecting her routine. And the bruises she received for her troubles. She's almost depleted my supplies of magical healing ointment."

"You know what they say," Krystal said, floating with all the compliments. "No pain, no gain."

Suddenly, a messenger ran up, panting for breath. "Your majesty," he said, "I have an urgent letter from Roark Fortress."

Queen Heart frowned. "I fear this may be bad news," she said. "King Talfren has been ill for weeks. Come, we will read it in private."

"Can I come, too?" Princess Serafina asked.

Queen Heart shook her head. "No," she replied. "You must stay here and enjoy the festivities. The people are your first priority today. They have come to watch your birthday celebrations and to see you."

"Yes, mother," Serafina said. She was clearly disappointed, but she didn't argue.

The Riders and Jala followed the sweep of Queen Heart's skirts out of the marquee, across the lawn, and into the palace. She led them into a small room. "We won't be disturbed here," said Queen Heart.

The Queen broke the letter's waxed seal, which bore the image of a griffin, the magical creature native to Haartsfeld.

Krystal held her breath, wondering what news the letter contained.

• CHAPTER 2 •

"IT IS AS I FEARED," Queen Heart said as she dropped the letter in her lap. "King Talfren passed away two days ago."

"How terrible," Quinn said, dabbing her eyes.

Willow shook her head. "Talfren was a great ruler," she said.

"And a valuable ally against Lord Valerian," Queen Heart said. "We've always been able to count on Talfren in battles against our nasty Obeerian neighbor. I fear for Haartsfeld now that Talfren is gone."

"Who's next in line to the throne?" Krystal asked. "Are there any heirs?"

"There is one," Queen Heart replied. "And in this letter from King Talfren, his last dying wish is that the Unicorn Riders find that heir."

"Why do we have to find the heir?" Krystal asked. "We're not Haartsfeldians."

"Many believe Talfren's heir is hiding in Avamay," Jala said. "She is half-Avamayan, after all."

Ellabeth rubbed her forehead. "Can someone please explain what's happening?" she asked. "You're all talking in riddles."

Jala chuckled. "Who knows Haartsfeldian history and can bring Ellabeth up to speed?" she asked.

Quinn, who loved history, put up her hand. "I know, a little," she said.

"Go ahead," Jala said.

Quinn chewed her lip. "Okay, um, many years ago when Talfren was a young prince, he went searching through the eight kingdoms for a wife," Quinn explained. "After years of traveling, he hadn't met anyone suitable. No one he loved."

"On his way home, he passed through Ingawan, the great forest northeast of here, where he was attacked by a bear," Quinn went on. "Prince Talfren was so badly injured that people thought he might die. A young fairy woman called Dalissa happened upon the prince's travel party. Seeing how sick he was, she helped him back to her home and cared for him until he was well again. During this time, Prince Talfren fell in love with Dalissa. He refused to return home unless she agreed to marry him."

"How sweet," Ellabeth said sighing.

"Did Dalissa marry the prince?" Willow asked.

Quinn nodded. "She did," she said, "but it was a huge sacrifice for her to leave Ingawan."

"Isn't love worth any sacrifice?" Ellabeth said dreamily.

"I didn't know you were a romantic," Krystal said, giggling.

Ellabeth rolled her eyes. "That's what I've heard," she said. "I don't really know."

"It's difficult for fairies to live in the human world," Quinn continued. "Their magical powers are weakened when they're away from their homes and family, both of which they are very much tied to."

"Has Lord Valerian ever managed to capture any?" Krystal asked. "He usually likes to destroy magical creatures so they can pose no threat to him."

"Thankfully, no," Jala said. "The Ingawan fairies live a reclusive life. It's possible Lord Valerian may not have even heard of them."

Willow tapped her chin. "For the fairies' sake, I sure hope that's true," she said.

"Getting back to the romance," Ellabeth prompted. "Did Talfren and Dalissa live happily ever after?"

"They did at first," Quinn replied. "They even had a daughter, Aveena."

"The heir," Krystal guessed.

"Yes," Quinn said. "Dalissa tried to be a good queen and mother, but she missed her home terribly. Not even baby Aveena made her truly happy. Eventually, Dalissa faded away." Quinn sniffed sadly. "The king was heartbroken, of course. He refused to remarry. That's why there are no other heirs."

"There is the king's younger brother, Duke Bowral," Jala said.

"That man is not fit to be king," Queen Heart said. "He is cruel and selfish. He will squeeze the lifeblood out of Haartsfeld and the people if he takes the throne. King Talfren told me he often had to intervene in his brother's affairs for the sake of some poor servant or villager, to save her job or her life."

"What about Aveena?" Krystal asked. "Where is she now?"

"No one knows, do they, Jala?" Quinn said.

"Not for certain," Jala agreed. "There were rumors Duke Bowral had Aveena murdered because he

19

desired his brother's crown so badly. But there was never any proof to support this claim. King Talfren believed the fairies stole her and took her back to Ingawan. Although King Talfren searched, he never found her."

Tears pricked Krystal's eyes. How dreadful for King Talfren not to know where his daughter was, she thought. And now Aveena will never see him again.

"How long has she been missing?" Krystal asked.

"Almost five years," Jala said.

"That would make her ten now," Queen Heart said.

"Young to be a queen," Willow observed. "Is Aveena really our best hope?"

"She may be half-fairy, but she's also half-human and therefore half-Haartsfeldian," Queen Heart said. "And she is a royal, whether she acknowledges it or not. Her ability to rule lies within her. It just needs to be awakened. If Aveena is anything like her father, she will always have the best interests of her people at heart."

"We can't let the Haartsfeldians suffer under Duke Bowral," Willow said. "We have to fulfill King Talfren's dying wish and find his daughter. Or at least give it a good try."

Queen Heart smiled. "I knew I could count on your bravery and sense of justice, Willow," she said. "So, girls, you have a mission. You must ride to Ingawan Forest and locate the lost princess. I hope with all my heart you can find her and convince her to accompany you to Roark Fortress to take up the throne. But you must hurry. By Haartsfeldian law, if Talfren's closest living heir is not crowned within three more days — a total of five days after his death — Duke Bowral can seize the throne. All claim Aveena has will be erased."

"So, we have three days to find Aveena and get her to Roark," Krystal said.

"Yes," said Jala.

"Alright, Riders," Willow said. "Start preparing the unicorns. Do we ride as one?"

"We ride as one!" they cheered.

• CHAPTER 3 •

THE RIDERS SET OUT from Keydell immediately. They had no time to waste so they used Fayza's speed magic. Golden sparks whirled from her horn, enveloping the Riders and their unicorns and helping them travel faster.

"Would you want to be a princess against your will?" Quinn asked Krystal as they galloped along.

Krystal laughed. "You'd never have to force me to be a princess," she said. The wind streamed through her long hair, making it fly behind her like a golden river. "I'd love to be one. Imagine getting your own way all the time."

"Being a princess could never compare to being a Unicorn Rider," Ellabeth said. "Nothing beats our adventurous life. Serafina always misses out on the action."

"She has her royal duties instead," Willow said.

"Which would be rather tedious, I'd say," Ellabeth said. "Think of all the battle strategies and customs and proper manners you'd have to learn. Plus you'd always have to be kind and fair and generous to everyone."

"I didn't realize you knew what that word meant," Krystal said.

"What, 'generous'?" Ellabeth asked.

"No." Krystal laughed, teasing her friend. "I wasn't aware you knew what 'manners' were."

Ellabeth poked her tongue out. "Ha-ha," she said.

"You're right, though," Krystal admitted. "Being a Unicorn Rider is better than being a princess. Still, it doesn't hurt imagining a different life for a while."

"It doesn't appeal to me," Ellabeth said.

Willow agreed. "I'm happy being a Rider," she said.

"Me, too," Quinn said, although she seemed uncertain.

It was twilight when they reached Ingawan Forest. Ancient conifers towered above them as they trotted into the cool shadows. The scent of damp earth and pine needles flooded their senses.

"Don't you love that smell?" Willow asked.

"Reminds me of snowy afternoons by the fire," Krystal said.

"You can't blame Aveena for wanting to live here," Quinn said, gazing all around. "It's so peaceful. And pretty."

"What if we can't find Aveena?" Ellabeth asked. "Or she doesn't want to be found? Ingawan is vast. She could be anywhere."

Magic began to swirl from Ula's horn as she mind-messaged Quinn.

"Ula says we're being watched," Quinn said.

The Riders immediately halted their unicorns. Krystal and the others dismounted and scanned the forest.

"We must find Aveena no matter what," Willow said loudly, as if she wanted to be overheard. "We have important news for her, remember?"

A rustling sound came from behind the trees.

"We know you're there," Krystal shouted. "Don't be afraid. We're friendly."

Branches parted and out stepped the most unusual combination of characters Krystal had ever seen. A boy came first, followed by a bear, a badger, and a skunk.

A skunk? Krystal thought, squinting to make sure the twilight wasn't playing tricks on her. *I can't stand those things. They're so smelly!*

Quinn gasped. Krystal squeezed her hand reassuringly. Willow called the unicorns over so the Riders could shield them from the strangers.

"Are you a fairy?" Willow asked.

"I am," said the boy. He was short and thin and had pointed ears. His bare arms were sculpted with fine muscles. He was barefoot and wore a sleeveless, knitted tunic tied at the waist. His almond-shaped eyes sparkled against his dark skin. "I'm Boyce. Did you say you were looking for Aveena?"

"We are," Willow said. "Is the bear trustworthy?"

Boyce's chin lifted. "He's as trustworthy as a Unicorn Rider," he replied.

"So you know who we are?" Krystal said.

"I've heard stories," Boyce said, shrugging his shoulders. "I always thought the tales were made up to amuse us children. Now I know you're real."

The badger grunted and twitched its nose.

"Badger wants to know if you've got any food," Boyce said.

Willow checked her pack. She handed Boyce some bread. "It's all we have left," Willow said. "We were hoping to hunt for more food should we need it."

"Thanks," Boyce replied. "It'll do."

Krystal expected Boyce to eat the bread. He was so thin, after all. Instead, he split the loaf into three uneven parts. One large, one medium, and one small. He handed the large piece to the bear, who quickly swallowed it. The badger got the middle-sized piece and proceeded to gnaw on it. The skunk took the smallest piece in its tiny black paws and nibbled daintily.

Krystal was impressed by the boy's selflessness. He obviously cared for his animal friends.

"Can you take us to Aveena?" Willow asked. "We need to speak to her right away."

Boyce tilted his head as if listening to something. "Follow me," he said.

The Riders guided their unicorns through the forest after the fairy boy and his animal companions.

Krystal kept her eyes peeled. *You can never be too careful when it comes to strangers,* she reminded herself.

"Do you think we can trust him?" Krystal whispered to Willow as they traipsed deeper into the forest.

"I've heard fairies are a playful bunch and Boyce might be up to anything," Willow said. "Right now we don't have any choice but to see where he's taking us. Stay close and let's hope for . . ."

Before Willow could finish her sentence, the Riders were surrounded. A hundred or more fairies appeared aiming sharp spears and lethal arrows directly at them.

Krystal noted that the biggest fairies weren't much taller than a ten year old, though many appeared much older. They were all barefoot, like Boyce, with the same pointed ears, and dark skin and hair. Their sparkling, mischievous eyes were caramel-colored with amazingly long lashes.

We've been tricked, Krystal silently fumed. She was about to tell Estrella to use her enchantment magic, but Willow signaled for her to remain calm.

"Hand over your unicorns or die," Boyce commanded.

Krystal glanced at the other Riders. She knew by their determined looks and set jaws they would never agree to Boyce's order. Neither would she.

"We can't do that," Willow said.

"Then prepare to die!" Boyce shouted as the fairies attacked.

• CHAPTER 4 •

ELLABETH LEAPED ONTO FAYZA and whirled her lasso, trying to catch as many fairies as she could. But they were too elusive and simply danced around the rope. Hordes of fairies jumped down from the trees. They quickly overcame Ellabeth and tied her wrists and ankles with vines. Fayza was chased into a makeshift yard where she was locked away. Ellabeth screamed with rage.

Willow and Obecky charged toward the fairies in an attempt to force them back into the forest. But the creatures stood their ground and kept their sharp spears aimed at Obecky's chest.

"Unless you want your unicorn injured, you'll dismount immediately," one of the fairies told Willow.

31

Willow had no choice but to obey. She stood silently while she was also tied up. Obecky was quickly chased into the yard beside Fayza.

Quinn used her trick-riding skills to evade capture in the narrow confines of the forest. But when Boyce's bear burst through the trees, roaring at her with bared teeth, Quinn was so frightened she toppled to the ground. After being momentarily lost from view beneath a swarm of fairies, Quinn

resurfaced with her hands and feet bound. Tears streamed down her face as she apologized to Ula for allowing her to be caught.

Krystal had the most success, using Estrella's enchantment magic. The fairies fell into a trance as they were dazzled by Estrella. They almost gave up their weapons, but Estrella struggled to control so many fairies as more and more of them dropped down from the trees to join the fight.

The unicorn's magic lost its effect and Krystal was quickly caught.

All four Riders were soon hanging upside down from a branch, trussed up like turkeys for the chopping block.

"So much for hoping for the best," Krystal said, glaring at the forest floor.

"Wait until I get my hands on that boy," Willow seethed, her cheeks flushed with anger. "Taking our last scrap of food then tricking us. It's not right."

The unicorns whinnied. A tight knot of worry formed in Krystal's stomach. She struggled against the vines. It was no use. She was stuck fast.

Boyce, flanked by several fairies, approached the Riders with a confident swagger.

"I like her," one of the tiny villains said, poking Krystal with his spear. "She's pretty."

More fairies crowded around Krystal. They tugged at her hair and ran their fingers through it, grasping it with delight.

"Liquid gold," they said. "How is it possible?"

"It's hair," Krystal said. "Now stop that, you're hurting me." If she hadn't been tied up she would have slapped their hands away.

"Quiet!" one of the fairies commanded. Krystal guessed he was the leader. His voice boomed with authority as he strode toward them wearing a crown of purple and white primroses.

"I am Woldeff," the fairy leader said. "Are you the Unicorn Riders?"

"Yes," Willow said. "We protect Avamay from evil forces. Which means we're your protectors, too."

"My name is Eera," a female fairy said, stepping forward. She wore a pure-white silk dress that shone like moonlight. Her raven-black hair curled to her waist. "What evil forces do you speak of?"

"Lord Valerian for one," Krystal said. "He's the ruler of Obeera, the country to the north of here. Have you never heard of him?"

"We don't know much about the outside world," Eera said.

"If you'd let us go, we could show you that we don't mean you any harm," Ellabeth said.

"Yes, please let us go," Krystal said. "We're feeling ill hanging upside down. This really is no way to treat visitors."

"We don't get many visitors," Woldeff said. "And we like it that way. So, we will untie only one of you." He pointed to Krystal. "You. Golden Hair. You may come and talk to me. The others shall remain here."

The vines uncoiled from around Krystal's ankles. She fell to the ground. "Please. Can my friends come, too?" she asked. "I can't bear to see them in pain."

"Your empathy is admirable," Woldeff said. "Vines, release the others, but they must stay here. I wish to talk to Golden Hair alone."

"Tell them why we're here," Willow urged Krystal. "And ask about Aveena."

"Right," Krystal said, glancing around for Woldeff. "Where did he go?"

Boyce pointed toward the forest canopy.

Krystal tipped her head back. "Oh, tree houses," she said. "How do I get up there?"

Boyce pointed to a vine hanging nearby.

"Good thing I know a bit about trapeze," Krystal said as she grabbed the vine and prepared to climb it. Before she could go anywhere, the vine had wrapped itself around her body.

"Hold on," Eera said.

The vine recoiled.

"Aaaaghhh!" Krystal shrieked as she shot upward.

The vine came to a jerky halt. Krystal was deposited onto a large timber platform. All around were tree houses of various shapes and sizes, camouflaged in the branches and leaves.

Candles burned in windows. Children ran and played together, along with birds, lizards, and squirrels.

Krystal stood marveling at the secret tree-top city until she felt a spear point prod her arm. "Don't keep Woldeff waiting," a fairy told her as he motioned toward a woven straw flap that served as a door to one of the houses. Krystal stepped inside.

The room was decorated with brightly-colored rugs and cushions scattered across the floor. A pot-belly stove sat in the corner, its higgledy-piggledy chimney poking through the roof.

"Sit," Woldeff commanded. "Tell me why you are here."

Krystal explained about the Riders' mission. "So you see," she finished, "it's crucial I speak to Aveena."

"What if Aveena does not wish to return to the world of humans?" Woldeff asked.

"She must," Krystal said. "Her people need her."

"What about her people here?" he said.

"You seem to have a good life," Krystal said. "But if Aveena doesn't return to Haartsfeld, her uncle, Duke Bowral, will seize the throne. From all accounts, the man isn't fit to be king."

"Uncle Woldeff," a girl's voice sounded from the corner. Krystal gave a start. She hadn't noticed anyone else in the room. *Had the girl been there all the time?*

"Yes, my child?" Woldeff said.

The girl stepped into the light. She was a good head taller than her uncle. Her outfit was neat and tidy, but her long hair was uncombed. Her hazel eyes — not caramel like the others — were wild with fury.

Is that Aveena? Krystal wondered. *I never would have guessed this girl was a princess.*

"I won't go," the girl said, stomping her foot. "And no one can make me."

"Even though it was your father's dying wish that you return to Roark?" Woldeff asked.

Aveena's eyes filled with tears. "Of course I'm upset my father died," she said. "But I can't leave here. I can't." She shot out the door.

Krystal chased after her. "Wait!" she yelled.

Aveena leaped into thin air. Krystal gasped, thinking the girl would fall to her death. Instead, a vine whipped out to catch her. Krystal watched her swing away through the trees.

"You have to do something," Krystal pleaded with Woldeff.

The fairy leader stared into the night. "It's out of my hands," he said.

● CHAPTER 5 ●

"IT'S NO USE," Krystal told the others. "Aveena won't leave Ingawan."

It was the following morning. The Riders and their unicorns had been reunited. They had spent the night sleeping on the forest floor and were still under the close watch of numerous fairy guards.

"You have to convince her to change her mind," Willow said as she glanced over her shoulder to make sure she wasn't overheard.

"Why me?" Krystal asked.

"Because you've met her already," Quinn said. "We don't even know what she looks like."

"Plus, the fairies like you," Ellabeth added. "Or at least your hair. All that brushing has finally been worth it."

"Very funny," Krystal said as she flicked her long hair back.

Willow fixed Krystal with a steady gaze. "This all comes down to you, Krystal," Willow said. "It's your responsibility to get Aveena to come with us. And when she does, she'll be your charge. If she's going to give up her home, she'll need someone to depend on, someone to talk to, and someone to help her. Are you okay with that?"

Krystal gulped. *I've never had to look after anyone before,* she thought. *What if I don't know what to do?*

"It'll be good for you," Ellabeth said. "Just think of Aveena like a sister. Then it'll be easy."

"Um, I'm not sure," Krystal said hesitantly.

"You'll be fine," Quinn said. "All you have to do is be nice to her. I know you can do this."

Krystal felt a glow of pleasure. With her friends encouraging her, she knew she could do anything. "All right," she said. "I'll go."

Willow patted her back. "Great. Thanks," she said.

When the guards tried to stop her, Krystal signaled for Estrella to use her enchantment magic. The unicorn reared onto her back legs and twirled around in circles like a dancer. Pearly-white magic spun from her horn, weaving around the guards. A dazed look came over their faces. They grinned as they dropped their spears and stared off into the distance, as if in a daze.

While Estrella's magic held the fairies in a stupor, Krystal slipped away into the forest. She searched everywhere for Aveena, in the tree houses and on the ground. She asked any fairies who would talk to her if they knew where Aveena was. Most seemed more interested in touching Krystal's hair than talking to her.

Finally, Krystal found a fairy girl who claimed to know where Aveena was.

"This way," the girl said as she led Krystal to a stream. She pointed. "There."

Krystal strained her eyes. As she watched, she was able to make out minute movements until finally the figure of Aveena emerged from the shapes and shadows of the forest. She was sitting with her back to Krystal and was bent over something.

"I didn't see her at first," Krystal said. "But she was there all the time."

The girl smiled. "That's the fairy magic," she said. "We blend in so others don't see us."

Krystal glanced down to reply, but the girl had vanished.

Krystal walked toward Aveena, not wanting to startle her. She peered over her shoulder and saw she was carving something from a piece of wood.

"What is it?" Krystal asked.

Aveena didn't look up. "Nothing," she said.

"It's beautiful. Is it a bird?" Krystal asked.

"It's an owl, my fairy totem," Aveena said. "Don't you know anything?"

"I didn't know fairies had symbols like Unicorn Riders," Krystal said.

"Well they do," Aveena replied. 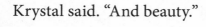 "My owl stands for wisdom and truth."

"My diamond symbol stands for wisdom, too," Krystal said. "And beauty."

"You are beautiful. That's obvious," Aveena said. She didn't sound as if she meant it as a compliment. Krystal decided to give her the benefit of the doubt.

"Thanks," Krystal said. "That's nice of you to say. Is Boyce's totem the bear?"

Aveena gave a curt nod. "He rescued the bear from a trap when he was very young," she said. "Those two are inseparable."

"And the badger and the skunk?" Krystal asked.

"They're his friends," Aveena said. "Boyce is always helping animals. That's why I like him."

Krystal sat beside Aveena, watching her carve. "You know, it's okay to be afraid," she said eventually.

"I'm not afraid," replied Aveena.

"Then why won't you come to Haartsfeld?" Krystal asked.

"Because I don't want to," Aveena said. "This is my home. I love it here."

"Give it a try. You might love Haartsfeld, too," Krystal persisted.

"I lived there before and hated it. So did my mother," said Aveena.

"She loved your father enough to give up this life," Krystal said.

Aveena grumbled vaguely in reply.

Some manners would go a long way with this one, Krystal thought. *A royal should always be courteous, just like Queen Heart.*

Krystal decided to try again. "Aveena, the people of Haartsfeld need you," she said. "This is your chance to do something positive, something worthwhile."

"Me?" Aveena asked in a tiny voice.

"Yes, you," Krystal said. She looked at Aveena with a steady gaze, knowing that what she said now could make a difference to the future of Haartsfeld. "You're the king's daughter. The rightful heir to the throne. I don't know if you remember your uncle, Duke Bowral, but from what I've heard, he's cruel and nasty. He's also determined to steal your throne from you. He doesn't deserve it, Aveena!

"Queen Heart knew your father and respected him as a king and a leader," Krystal went on. "She believes *you're* the best person to inherit the throne from him. And I trust my queen with all my heart, which is why I'm here, pleading with you to do the right thing."

Aveena coughed. "When you put it like that . . . ," she said. Her voice was a whisper, her eyes downcast. "How can I not agree? Fine, I'll go. But first, we must tell Woldeff. He'll be upset to see me leave."

Aveena was right, Woldeff was far from happy with her decision.

"If we are to lose you, it will be a great sacrifice," he said, addressing the Unicorn Riders. "The fairy people must have some repayment for the loss of Aveena, our cherished one. Who among you is willing to make this sacrifice?"

Willow stepped forward. "As Head Rider, I'll be happy to," she said. "Tell me what you want and it will be done."

After a heated discussion with several other fairies, Woldeff replied, "We want nothing from you, Head Rider. However, there is another who can offer us something special we cannot obtain here." He pointed to Krystal.

"W-what do I have that you want?" Krystal stammered.

"Your hair," Eera said. "We could weave beautiful things from it and use it to develop our magic. Already, I have ideas for creating new blending cloaks and dream catchers. Will you let us have it?"

Krystal was horrified. "My hair?" she asked.

Woldeff clasped his hands together. "That is all we ask in return for our beloved Aveena, the Haartsfeldian queen-in-waiting," he said. "It is a small price to pay, is it not?"

• CHAPTER 6 •

KRYSTAL WANTED TO STOMP her foot like Aveena had. Asking for her hair was so personal. How dare they! It had taken years to grow her hair. She loved her golden locks so much, she wasn't sure she could give them up.

"You can't have my hair," Krystal said. "And that's final."

She turned and stalked into the forest, her fists bunched angrily at her sides.

I need to get away for a while to clear my mind, she told herself.

Krystal kept walking until she came to a clearing. Sunlight shone through a gap in the forest canopy. In the middle of the clearing stood a weeping willow. Its drooping, emerald branches cascaded to the ground. Krystal pushed the branches apart and crawled inside. She bent her head and cried softly. Krystal's long, golden hair fell over her face, hiding it just as the willow's long leaves hid her within their green folds.

The next thing Krystal knew, she was being shaken. She rubbed her eyes and saw Willow, Ellabeth, and Quinn huddled around her with worried faces.

"Are you okay?" Quinn asked as she rubbed Krystal's shoulders.

"We thought you were lost," Ellabeth said.

"Sorry," Krystal mumbled. "It was silly to take off. I was just upset."

"We understand," Willow said. "It's not every day you're asked to give up something important."

"Or something you love," Krystal said.

That's when the truth hit her. *This is how Aveena must feel,* she realized. *The poor girl . . . But I'm a Unicorn Rider. It's up to me to set an example.*

Krystal rose and brushed the grass from her uniform. She met Willow's eyes with a determined look. "I've decided to let them have my hair," she said.

Quinn stopped her. "You don't have to do this," she said.

"Yes, I do," replied Krystal. "It's a small price to pay for Haartsfeld's safety. If Aveena can give up her freedom, I can give up my hair."

"If it makes you feel better, you can brush my hair whenever you like," Ellabeth joked.

"Strangely enough, that is actually some consolation," Krystal said, giving a wobbly smile. "Even if it will only be to hear you screech as I pull the knots out."

The four friends laughed as they walked back to the fairy village. When they arrived, they let the vines whirl them up to the tree houses.

"Golden Hair, you have returned," Woldeff said. "Does this mean . . . ?"

"I'm ready," Krystal said.

"Do you give your hair of your own free will?" Eera asked. "It will be useless in our magic unless you do."

"Yes," Krystal said. "Now let's do this before I change my mind."

Eera helped Krystal into a nearby chair. As Eera cut Krystal's hair with shiny silver scissors, Quinn held her friend's hand. Silent tears fell down Krystal's cheeks as her golden locks slid to the floor.

When it was over, Eera raised Krystal's hair in the air. The fairies burst into applause, dancing and cheering.

At least they appreciate my gift, Krystal thought sadly.

Willow and Ellabeth hugged her. Quinn held up a mirror so Krystal could see herself. She turned her head this way and that, wondering at the strange girl in the mirror. "I look so different," she said.

"You look sweet," Quinn said. "It suits you."

"Really?" Krystal asked.

"Really," Ellabeth reassured her.

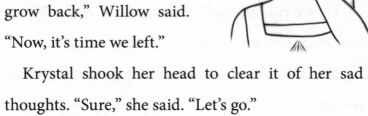

"And don't worry, it'll grow back," Willow said. "Now, it's time we left."

Krystal shook her head to clear it of her sad thoughts. "Sure," she said. "Let's go."

But when the Riders dropped down to the ground to get the unicorns, they found Aveena grumpy and uncooperative. "I can't find Boyce," she complained. "And I'm not leaving without saying goodbye to him."

"Come on, Aveena, ride on Estrella with me," Krystal said. "You'll love it, I promise." She threw Estrella a wink.

Estrella nickered softly then sent a burst of enchantment magic floating over Aveena. The fairy stared at Estrella in wonder, not realizing she was being entranced by the pearly-white sparks. When Krystal saw Aveena's resistance dissolve, she jumped onto Estrella and held her hand out. Aveena took it eagerly, climbed up behind Krystal and put her hands around her waist.

"Do we ride as one?" Willow asked as the Riders mounted their unicorns.

"We ride as one!" the girls cried in unison as they set out.

"Do you remember Haartsfeld at all?" Krystal asked Aveena as they rode along. "Is it much different from Avamay?"

"There are mountains everywhere," Aveena said. "And cliffs and ravines and rocks. I hate rocks. Give me trees or grass any day."

"You'll get used to rocks eventually," Willow said.

Aveena shrugged. "I guess," she replied.

Ula nickered nervously.

"What's wrong, Ula?" Quinn said. "Do you sense trouble?"

Quinn's face paled. "She said there's danger ahead," said Quinn.

"Where?" Krystal asked, looking around.

Suddenly, a cluster of rocks flew at them.

Obecky whinnied and reared on her back legs.

"Ouch!" Willow cried as she was struck on the arm. "Riders, take cover!"

• CHAPTER 7 •

A ROAR SOUNDED THROUGH the trees, followed by the appearance of a shaggy brown bear hurtling on all fours toward the Riders, snarling and snapping. On its back sat Boyce, rapidly firing rocks from his slingshot. Behind them came the badger and the skunk, grunting angrily.

Krystal was struck on the leg and head by rocks. With a cry of delight at the sight of Boyce, Aveena fearlessly stood up on Estrella's back and leaped into her friend's arms. The pair would have ridden off together if it hadn't been for Ellabeth's quick thinking. Using Fayza's speed magic, she galloped after them, whipping her lasso out and throwing it with precision. The rope flew over Boyce and

Aveena's heads and then dropped around their waists. Ellabeth drew the lasso tight.

The bear disappeared into the trees with the badger close on its heels. Boyce and Aveena were pulled up short. They fell to the ground, still caught in Ellabeth's lasso. Boyce looked shocked. Aveena's fists were clenched by her sides, and her eyes were hard with fury.

Terrified by the noise, the skunk sprayed its horrid scent. The Riders scattered. Krystal didn't move quickly enough and was covered in the dreadful smell. She squealed and swatted at her uniform, trying to rid it of the skunk's smell.

"Brilliant rescue plan," Aveena grunted at Boyce. "Untie me now, Riders."

"Not until you promise not to do anything foolish," Ellabeth said.

"Anything *more* foolish, that is," Willow corrected her.

"You'll have to take that up with Boyce," Aveena said as she wrestled with the lasso. "This was his idea."

"We made a pact with your people," Krystal said, glaring at Boyce. "I gave up my hair in return for the fairies giving Aveena up and her cooperating. This stunt goes against that pact."

"But I'll miss her if she goes," Boyce said. His voice was tight with emotion.

Krystal could tell he was trying not to cry. She felt his sadness and his honesty. She untied the lasso and helped them both to their feet. "So that's why you cooked up this ridiculous ambush?" Krystal asked.

Boyce nodded. "I don't want to lose my best friend," he said.

"Yuck, what's that horrible stench?" Ellabeth interrupted, screwing up her nose.

Krystal winced. "It's nothing. I'll have it sorted in a few minutes," she replied.

"Oh dear," Quinn sighed. "It's skunk spray. You're covered in it," she said.

Krystal went and sat on a nearby log. "This is not my lucky day," said Krystal.

"Hey, what's this?" Ellabeth asked. With one hand pinching her nose, she used her other hand to gently inspect Krystal's head. "You've got a nasty gash here. Thanks to one of Boyce's rocks, no doubt."

Willow took a closer look. "Obecky will fix that," she said. "It might be tender for a few days, but her magic will clean the wound and help it heal faster."

Krystal sat quietly while Obecky worked her magic. Blue-gray sparkles shot from Obecky's horn and shimmered all around Krystal's wound. They helped cleanse and seal the cut.

"That was incredible," Boyce said when she finished. "The cut's almost gone. What else can unicorns do?"

"Lots of things," Willow said. "They're as special to Avamay as fairies are. We often use their magic to help us on our missions."

Ula nickered.

"What is it, girl?" Quinn asked. She concentrated while Ula mind-messaged her.

"Is something wrong?" Willow asked.

63

Quinn gulped. "Here, I'll show you," she said, turning to Ellabeth. "Can you ask Fayza to focus her light magic up here?" She pointed above their heads. "If I concentrate hard, I might be able to project what Ula is seeing into Fayza's magic so you can see, too. It will show everyone what's happening in Haartsfeld right now and why Aveena's people need her so badly. Duke Bowral is up to no good, I'm afraid."

Fayza whirled her magic into a golden orb above the Riders' heads. Quinn rested one hand on Ula's forehead and then reached her other hand deep inside the orb. Images flickered across the bright, magical ball. They saw images of homes and shops set ablaze; of women and children running terrified and screaming through the streets; of soldiers on muscular warhorses pursuing unarmed men.

Aveena shuddered. "Those poor people. I didn't realize," she said.

"Me either," Boyce admitted. "Will Aveena be safe in Haartsfeld? It looks scary."

"You're afraid for Aveena, aren't you?" Krystal asked. "You're afraid we won't be able to protect her."

Boyce hesitated a moment before replying. "I overheard you talking about how dangerous it was in Haartsfeld," he said. "I couldn't bear it if anything happened to Aveena." He glanced at his friend. Aveena blushed self-consciously.

"We won't let anything harm her," Krystal said.

"And we won't leave her at Roark Fortress unless we're certain she will be safe," Ellabeth added. "We want peace to reign throughout every kingdom. Not war. We won't let Duke Bowral threaten Aveena or seize power in Haartsfeld."

"I've been selfish," Boyce told Aveena. "I wanted to keep you here because we have so much fun together. I didn't want you to leave."

The bear and the badger appeared beside Boyce and rumbled in agreement.

"But your people need you," Boyce continued. "I shouldn't try to make you stay."

"Come with me," Aveena said as she clung to her friend.

"I don't belong in Haartsfeld," Boyce said. "But you do. You have to help your people and take care of them, like Woldeff takes care of us." He gave Aveena a fierce hug and then jumped on the bear. "Goodbye, Aveena. Remember me well."

Boyce rode off. He didn't look back.

Aveena covered her face with her hands and sobbed.

"What should we do?" Quinn asked.

Willow glanced at the sky. "It's getting dark," she said. "We may as well camp here and give Aveena one final night with her beloved Ingawan. Tomorrow we'll enter Haartsfeld and there will be no turning back. Hopefully, stepping on home soil will revive Aveena's feelings of love for her other country."

"And if it doesn't?" Krystal asked.

"Then all of Haartsfeld will pay the price," Willow said.

• CHAPTER 8 •

KRYSTAL STAYED WITH AVEENA while the others searched for food. She kept busy lighting a fire and grooming Estrella while Aveena sat sulkily, refusing to help.

"Why don't we go for a walk?" Krystal suggested. "It might take your mind off things."

Aveena reluctantly agreed.

While they were walking, Aveena spotted some berries. "Yum, let's pick some," she said. She ran over to a bush, plucked the soft, juicy berries from the thorny branches and then dropped them into her shirt, which she held wide to catch the fruit.

"What sort of berries are they?" Krystal asked. "I've not seen them before."

"Just regular forest berries," Aveena said.

"Are they safe to eat?" Krystal asked.

"Of course," Aveena replied.

Krystal's mouth watered. "I'm so hungry I could eat them all now," she said. She studied the berries in her hand. There weren't that many. "But I'd better wait until we get back to camp. I'm sure Ellabeth will be starving like always, and there's no guarantee the others will find food. Let's head back."

They arrived at the same time as the others. Willow carried a supply of fresh pigeon eggs. Quinn was carrying handfuls of plump, white mushrooms, and Ellabeth had managed to find some salad leaves and herbs.

At dinner, Aveena quickly ate her share and then looked around for more. Krystal handed her the remaining food on her plate. Aveena wolfed that down, too.

When it came time to eat the berries, however, Aveena rubbed her stomach and shook her head. "Thanks, but I don't think I could fit another thing in," she said.

The Riders eagerly shared the berries.

"Yum! They're delicious," Ellabeth said. "So sweet and juicy."

Krystal reached for more. "Save some for me," she said, grabbing more berries.

Ula nickered and magical sparks whirled from her horn.

"Are you trying to mind-message me, girl?" Quinn asked as she rubbed her forehead. "Sorry, I can't make it out."

Krystal yawned. "I'm so sleepy," she said.

"Me, too," Ellabeth mumbled.

Hours later when Krystal woke, her head was pounding and her throat was parched. "What time is it?" Krystal asked. She sat up and saw the fire had gone out.

"What's going on?" Willow asked. "I've got a splitting headache."

"Same," Krystal said. "Here, have a drink." She handed Willow her water bottle and pointed into the distance where the sun was a thin orange line on the horizon. Dawn was approaching. "We've been asleep for hours."

Quinn and Ellabeth were also awake by now.

"Where's Aveena?" Willow asked.

Krystal peeled back the layers of Aveena's sleeping bag. "She's not here!" Krystal said.

"Do you think those berries might have been poisonous?" Ellabeth asked. "Or at least a little, um, overpowering? What sort of berries were they?"

"Aveena called them forest berries," Krystal said.

Ellabeth sprang to her feet. "Forest berries usually don't have that effect. I'd say it's too much of a coincidence that we fell asleep and Aveena went missing. Wouldn't you?" Ellabeth said.

Krystal was close to tears. "That girl is impossible," she said. "I have tried everything. I just can't reach her. She is such a brat."

"Don't let her break your determination or patience," Quinn said.

"It's too late for that," Krystal groaned. "I think I give up."

"You know, when you first arrived at Keydell you weren't much different than Aveena," Willow said.

"Excuse me?" Krystal bridled. "I've never gone more than a few hours without brushing my hair. I don't do mischievous things like giving people sleeping berries. And I'm neat and tidy, and I never stamp my foot or get angry."

"Ahem," Ellabeth said as she crossed her arms. "That's exactly what you just did."

Krystal appealed to Quinn. "I didn't stamp my foot, did I?" she asked.

Quinn winced. "I'm afraid you did," she said.

Krystal sighed and plopped down on the ground. She thought about when she had first become a Unicorn Rider. She'd been delighted to see her name in The Choosing Book. What girl wouldn't?

Everyone in her home town of Bellannia had been so proud of her.

Then the hard work had begun. She'd had to learn to live with the other girls, take on the rules and responsibilities of being a Rider, and get to know her unicorn, Estrella. Then, of course, there was the uniform. It had taken Krystal ages to get used to wearing it instead of silk dresses.

Now Krystal was truly happy being a Rider. She couldn't imagine being anything else. But there had been a time when that wasn't the case. If she was completely honest, Krystal knew exactly how Aveena felt.

"Okay, so I was a little spoiled at first," she admitted.

"Spoiled doesn't even begin to describe it," Ellabeth said, laughing. "You complained about everything."

"Becoming a Rider was a difficult change for me," Krystal said.

"Imagine how Aveena feels," Willow said. "She has to become a queen."

Krystal looked deep inside herself and realized the truth. She couldn't give up on Aveena. The other Riders hadn't given up on her, and look how far she'd come. Now more than ever, Aveena needed her help and support.

"You're right," Krystal said. She stood up with renewed conviction. "We have to find her."

"That's more like it," Willow said. "We're short on time so we'll split up. Krystal and Ellabeth, you search that way." She pointed east. "Quinn and I will go this way. We'll meet back here in one hour."

• CHAPTER 9 •

"AVEENA!" KRYSTAL CALLED. She and Ellabeth had been searching for Aveena for almost an hour with no luck. "Hey, look, there's a river." Krystal slid down off Estrella and ran toward the water. "It must have been raining recently. The river is full to its banks. And there's Aveena!"

In the middle of the waterway sat a moss-covered log. Clinging to it was a miserable-looking and bedraggled Aveena.

Krystal cupped her hands together. "Hold on. We're coming," she said.

"Please, hurry!" Aveena shouted back.

Krystal spotted thick vines hanging from nearby trees. She tied several together then wound them around her waist.

"That water is cold and murky and flowing way too quickly," Ellabeth pointed out. "You'll be swept away if you go in there, Krystal."

"I don't want to go in either, but it's our job to get her to Roark safely," Krystal said, handing Ellabeth the end of the makeshift vine rope. "Tie these around those trees. Nice and tight, please."

Estrella nickered nervously as Krystal removed her boots and uniform, leaving only her undershirt and leggings on.

"It's all right, girl," Krystal said as she patted Estrella. "I'll be back soon."

Once Ellabeth had secured the vines, Krystal plunged into the water. She swam hard against the current, arms reaching and legs kicking. The vines around her waist creaked and strained. When she

finally reached the log, Krystal tried to climb up onto it, but it was too slippery. As she slid back into the water, the vines snapped and were carried away by the current.

"Try again," Ellabeth said.

Krystal gripped the log so tightly that her fingers ached. Slowly and carefully, she pulled herself up out of the water. She crawled along the log until she reached Aveena. "Are you okay?" she asked, checking her for injuries.

Aveena's teeth chattered. Her skin was icy cold. "I'm sc-sc-scared," she said.

Krystal saw Aveena was holding something small and white. "What's that?" she asked.

"An owl," Aveena said, showing Krystal the bird. "Its wing is broken. I swam over to rescue it and then got stuck."

"We might have to leave it here," Krystal said.

"I told you before," Aveena said. "The owl is my totem. I have to save it."

Krystal thought for a moment. "Okay, the best way to do this is to perch the owl on your shoulder then wrap your arms around my neck and hold on tight," said Krystal. She stood up and called out to Ellabeth, "Will your lasso reach?"

"I'll give it a shot," Ellabeth replied. She twirled her lasso above her head and tossed it to Krystal.

The throw fell short.

"I'll come closer," Krystal said. She inched farther down the log.

Ellabeth tossed her lasso again. As Krystal reached out to grab it, she lost her footing and almost slipped into the water. "Yikes!" she exclaimed.

"Third time for luck," Ellabeth called. She threw her lasso straight and hard.

Krystal stretched her arms and caught the rope on the very tips of her fingers. "Right, this is it," she said. Krystal eased herself into the water with Aveena clinging to her back.

With the help of Fayza's speed magic, Krystal, Aveena, and the owl zoomed toward the shore. Ellabeth helped them out of the water.

"Willow and Quinn will be wondering where we are," Ellabeth said as she lit a fire to dry them out. "I'd better go find them."

As Ellabeth rode off on Fayza, Krystal sidled closer to Aveena. "Now, tell me about those forest berries," Krystal said.

"I didn't know the berries would make you sleepy," Aveena said as she wrung her hands together. "I thought they were the same ones we eat at home. When you all fell asleep, I realized I'd gotten mixed up. I ran away in case you got angry with me."

Krystal knew Aveena was telling the truth. She immediately softened. "How good are you at helping animals?" she asked.

"Very good," Aveena said, her eyes glowing.

The two girls worked together to set the owl's broken wing. All the while, Aveena talked to it in fairy language.

Aveena is good at this, Krystal thought. *She has a wonderful caring nature, despite her wild side. And that's a valuable skill for a queen to possess.*

"When Willow arrives, I'll ask her to use Obecky's healing magic to help him," Krystal said. "Would you like that?"

Aveena cradled the bird in her arms. "Yes," she said. "I'm going to call him Flutter."

"That's a nice name," Krystal said. "You were so brave trying to rescue him. Maybe that's how you should think of your role as queen. You'll be able to save lives and make a difference to so many people. You'll shine, I just know it."

Aveena's eyes widened with fear. "I don't want to shine. I want to be normal," she said. Tears splashed down her cheeks. "I'm going to miss Ingawan."

"Why don't you take it with you?" Krystal said.

Aveena looked puzzled. "How?" she asked.

Krystal untied the leather string around her neck. "This vial contains soil from Bellannia," said Krystal. "I've had it ever since I left home to become a Unicorn Rider. It's like a good luck charm. But I don't need it anymore. Not when I have Estrella."

Krystal undid the vial. She held it to her nose and breathed deeply. "Mmm, still smells like home," she said. She scattered the soil nearby, washed the bottle in the river, and then handed it to Aveena. "Put some soil or bark or leaves in there — whatever reminds you of Ingawan. Then, when you're feeling homesick, you'll always have it with you."

"I like that," Aveena said as she plucked leaves from a nearby oak tree. Then she collected some soil and pebbles from the riverbank and put them into the bottle. When the vial was full, she took a whiff of the contents inside. "It's exactly as you said, Krystal. You are wise, just like your totem."

"Thank heavens we found you," Willow said as she rode up with Ellabeth and Quinn. "Belmont, the Queen's messenger falcon, just delivered a message. Duke Bowral's army is marching toward Roark Fortress. We need to keep moving."

● CHAPTER 10 ●

THE RIDERS SET OFF with Aveena. Fayza's speed magic helped them race along. They quickly left Ingawan Forest behind and crossed the border into Haartsfeld. The terrain soon changed from thickly-wooded trees to rugged mountain ranges and barren, rocky valleys.

They came to a tiny village called Shah-on-Dee. The place appeared deserted. The streets were almost entirely empty. Anyone who was there wore black, the color of mourning. The Haartsfeldian flag, bearing the image of a griffin, flew at half-mast in the village square.

"They must have loved your father," Krystal told Aveena. "See how they mourn his death?"

"Yes," Aveena said solemnly.

"We need to stop and eat," Willow said. "We'll try this cottage." She pointed to a small house with roses growing in the garden.

A young woman came to the door bouncing a baby on her hip. "Oh, my. Unicorn Riders," she said. "I've heard about you."

Krystal smiled kindly. "We were hoping to rely on your hospitality for something to eat and drink," said Krystal. "We also have a special guest with us."

"Of course," the woman said. "What little I have is yours. Please, come in." She ushered them inside, telling them that her name was Pearl. She handed the baby to one of her older children then shooed them outside.

"It's been terrible losing our king," Pearl said. "And now Duke Bowral is planning to take over. We all know he's not fit to rule. If only someone else could take King Talfren's place." Pearl gazed out the window wistfully. "Oh, I am sorry. I've forgotten my manners." She paused to eye Aveena with her bare feet and messy hair. "Is this your special guest?"

Krystal nodded. "This is Aveena Tripleodian, heir to the Haartsfeldian crown," said Krystal.

Pearl blinked. "Oh!" she exclaimed. Her hand flew to her mouth. "I see it now. You have the King's eyes. Your majesty." She dropped into a deep curtsey.

"We're escorting Aveena to Roark for her coronation," Willow said. "But we can't present the future queen to court like this."

"Is there a seamstress in town?" Krystal asked.

"I'll fetch her right away," Pearl said.

"We need tomato juice, too," Ellabeth said. "About six jugs."

"Ellabeth!" Krystal gasped. "Are you thinking of your stomach again?"

"No." Ellabeth coughed. "It's the only thing that removes skunk scent."

Krystal was mortified. "Do I . . . ?" she said.

"Sorry, Krystal," Quinn said, giggling. "You do smell a little."

"Even after my dip in the river?" Krystal asked.

"You know skunk scent is almost impossible to get rid of," Willow said.

"Why didn't you say something?" Krystal asked.

Ellabeth shrugged. "I guess we were too polite," she said.

"That'll be the day," Krystal huffed.

Pearl hurried off. She soon returned with the tomato juice and the seamstress, Nessa, who began taking Aveena's measurements.

"You'll have to be careful with your skirts," Krystal told Aveena. "You're not used to wearing them long."

Aveena pouted. "Can't I wear long pants like you Riders?" she asked.

"I don't see why not," Willow said.

"Pants it is, then," Nessa said.

When Aveena proudly tried on the new clothes that Nessa had sewn, she saw a glimpse of the queen she might one day become.

"Wow, that's a huge improvement," Ellabeth said as Aveena gazed into the mirror. "And I mean huge!"

Aveena clenched her fists. "If I'm to be queen, it shouldn't matter how I look," she said. "People must accept me for who I am."

Krystal rushed to Aveena's side as Willow and Quinn steered Ellabeth outside.

"You're right, of course," Krystal said. "And people *will* accept you for who you are. They're going to love you. I just know it." She smiled. "Try not to feel too overwhelmed. When you arrive in Roark, you'll have tutors and advisors to assist you. It will get easier, trust me."

Aveena picked up Flutter, whispering to him. The owl flapped his wings.

"Obecky's magic seems to have worked," Krystal said. "His wing looks better. Perhaps we should let him go?"

Aveena clung to the bird. "Can't I keep him?" she asked.

"You know, that might be a good idea," Krystal said. "You two look like good friends already. It'll be nice for you to have a friend at Roark."

"I agree," Aveena said. Her face lightened for a moment before turning serious again. "Why did it have to be me?" She sighed. "I never asked for this."

"Sometimes we have to do things we don't want to do," Krystal said. "And that allows us to challenge ourselves or see the world in different ways. When we do, we become a better person. Or fairy. Now, come. It's time we took you to Roark."

"No," Aveena said, shaking her head. "It's not time."

Krystal's heart sank. Aveena still would not — could not — fulfill her duty. *We've failed our mission,* Krystal thought sadly. *I've failed.*

Aveena smiled. "Don't worry," she said. "I'm not going to run away again. What I mean is that it's *past* time I went to Roark. I've been hiding from my duty, my people, my future." She straightened her back, her hazel eyes shining. "I can't do that any more. You've made me see that it's right and truly time I became the queen my people need me to be."

Krystal was so relieved she wanted to squeal and cheer and jump up and down. Somehow, she managed to stay calm and only hugged Aveena instead. Then she raced outside to tell the other Riders they were ready to go.

• CHAPTER 11 •

THE UNICORN RIDERS AND Aveena galloped through the last rocky mountain pass leading to Roark Fortress. Ahead of them, they spotted Duke Bowral's men approaching from the east. Clouds of dust rose from behind the mounted horses and wagons.

"We're running out of time," Ellabeth said. "Aveena's three days to claim the throne are almost up. We've pushed the unicorns as hard as we can, and Duke Bowral is still going to beat us."

"We can't let him win," Krystal said. "We're almost there. Keep riding."

"Krystal's right," Willow said. "Ellabeth, can Fayza work her magic any harder to make us go faster?"

"Hold on. I'll ask her," Ellabeth replied. "Although she's pretty tired and has almost depleted her magic. Come on, girl," she encouraged Fayza. "You can do it."

Fayza responded valiantly, using every ounce of her strength to keep the group going. Moments later, the Riders came to a halt outside the fortress gates. Poor Fayza hung her head in exhaustion, her sides heaving.

Ellabeth slipped down off her back and patted her. "Well done, girl," she said. "You did it."

"Open up!" Willow shouted as she and the other Riders banged on the thick timber gate with their fists. "We have a special delivery."

A face appeared through a gap in the gate. "Who is it?" a gruff voice demanded.

"Willow Arkwright. Head Unicorn Rider from Avamay," said Willow. "Is it safe inside the fortress?"

"Aye," the voice replied. "For supporters of King Talfren, it is."

"Quick, Willow," Krystal said as she glanced over her shoulder. "Duke Bowral is right behind us and coming up fast. We must get Aveena inside."

"We have Talfren's daughter here," Willow told the gatekeeper. "We intend to see her crowned as queen."

"Talfren's daughter?" the gatekeeper asked.

The Riders heard several voices talking.

"Open the gate! Open the gate!" shouted voices from inside the fortress.

The huge gate swung open. The Riders were greeted by a sea of eager faces. Krystal helped Aveena down off Estrella. "It's her," the people of Haartsfeld said. "It's really her."

A tall, bearded man pushed through the crowd. "I'm General Savina, head of the king's army," he said, bowing to Aveena. "It is a pleasure to finally meet you, your majesty."

Aveena blushed. Her hand clutched at her throat, and her mouth flapped open and shut.

Krystal squeezed Aveena's hand reassuringly. "Princess Aveena is very pleased to meet you," Krystal said. "But I'm afraid we don't have time for formalities, General Savina. Duke Bowral is almost on your doorstep." She pushed Aveena through the gates. "Keep her safe."

"Of course," General Savina said. He motioned for some women to escort the princess inside. "We have made preparations for the coronation. We've been waiting and hoping these last three days that you Riders would come." General Savina turned to Aveena. "I was with the king when he died. I know how much he wanted you to be queen. The Haartsfeldian people are relieved you've made it."

"Not all of you seem relieved," Ellabeth said, nodding meaningfully toward Duke Bowral's approaching army.

"We must speak with Duke Bowral and tell him that his right to the throne no longer exists now that Aveena is here," Willow said.

"Wait," General Savina said as he reached out a hand to stop her. "Duke Bowral has managed to divide the king's army. Some of our men, even those

who were once faithful soldiers, have joined forces with him. I can guarantee he won't want to talk to you. You'll need our help if you wish to defeat him."

"Very well," Willow said. "Will you ride with us?"

A cheer of agreement rose from the crowd.

"I think you have your answer," General Savina said. "Riders, you lead and we'll follow."

It soon became clear that Duke Bowral had no intention of stopping to talk. The Riders were still

quite some distance from him when the air filled with arrows and spears. They were forced to take cover behind a group of rocks that dotted the landscape.

"Step aside or die!" the duke cried as he stood defiantly behind a line of his soldiers.

"In the name of all that is good and true," Willow replied, "we ask you to give up your claim to the throne. As we speak, Princess Aveena, King Talfren's daughter, is being crowned Queen of Haartsfeld. It's over, Duke Bowral."

"I will claim the Haartsfeldian throne for myself if I must," he replied. Duke Bowral lifted his arm, signaling for his men to attack. They ran forward, yelling and firing arrows.

Duke Bowral's words sickened Krystal. Queen Heart was right, she realized. This man should never be king. And it's up to us to stop him.

"I did try to warn you," General Savina said. He stood up and blew on the curved horn he carried in his belt. In response, his men charged to meet Duke Bowral's army.

"We must end this quickly," Willow said. "I can't bear to see men hurt for no reason. Riders, you know what to do."

The girls urged their unicorns forward. Willow and Quinn attacked the left flank together, on Obecky and Ula. Ellabeth rode to the right on Fayza, skirting around to the edge of the battling soldiers.

Fayza was still tired. She couldn't go as fast as usual. Ellabeth made up for it with her expertise using the lasso, whirling it high in the air then releasing it over groups of soldiers and pulling them to the ground. General Savina's men then moved in to disarm them.

Krystal saw that General Savina's soldiers were overcoming Duke Bowral's army.

The duke was furious. "Fight, you lazy dogs," he roared. "Or I will have you all jailed."

"Now, E!" Krystal said. She signaled to Estrella as she charged straight for him.

Sparks of magic swirled from Estrella's horn, enveloping Duke Bowral in a pearly-white cloud.

"Excellent aim, girl," Krystal said as she hugged Estrella's neck.

Duke Bowral stopped shouting orders. He kneeled on the ground, staring up at Estrella with glazed eyes. "I have seen the most beautiful sight in all the world," he murmured.

Willow whistled as she rode up with Quinn and Ellabeth. "He's a goner," she said.

"He sure is," Quinn said. "Well done, Krystal."

With their leader enchanted, Duke Bowral's army soon surrendered. General Savina thanked the Riders for their help. "You girls have done enough for today," he said. "We have things under control here. Why don't you head back to the fortress and see how our new queen is?"

Krystal grinned. "I'd like that very much," she said.

• CHAPTER 12 •

THE UNICORN RIDERS WAITED in a large room where the walls were lined with gold and the ceiling was painted with images of mythical creatures. The floorboards had been polished until they shone, and thick, richly-colored rugs lay here and there.

"This is much fancier than what I was expecting," Krystal said.

"Bigger, too," Quinn observed, tipping her head back to study the ceiling.

A door opened. Aveena strode in wearing a glittering silver-and-diamond tiara and flanked by four ladies-in-waiting dressed in silk dresses. "Riders!" she cried. "I heard all about what you did. Thank you so much."

"You're wearing a crown. Does that mean your coronation ceremony took place?" Krystal asked hopefully.

Aveena's hand flew to her head. She whisked the crown off. "This silly thing," said Aveena. She tossed the crown to one of the women who managed to catch it before it hit the floor. There was a sharp intake of breath from all four ladies-in-waiting. "That's going to take a bit of getting used to." She smiled at the Riders. "And yes, the coronation took place. You're looking at the new Queen of Haartsfeld."

"Congratulations!" Krystal said. She ran to hug Aveena. "Oh, I'm sorry." She blushed. "I shouldn't have done that. Forgive me, your majesty."

"Don't be silly," Aveena said. "I'd like a hug from all of you." She looked momentarily shy. "If you don't mind."

The Riders took turns hugging the child-queen. "It's a big day for you," Willow said.

"Do you feel any different?" Ellabeth asked. "Now that you're queen?"

"Not yet," Aveena said thoughtfully. "I don't think it's really hit me yet."

There was scratching at the door. A boy stumbled in carrying Flutter. "Ah, your majesty, he seems unsettled," he said. The boy tried to hold the bird as it shrieked and batted its wings wildly.

"Let him go," Aveena said. She held out her arm. Flutter flew across the room, his wings moving silently. He swooped down to land on Aveena's arm.

The ladies-in-waiting ducked low to avoid the bird's wings and talons.

"Don't worry, he won't hurt you," Aveena said.

The women didn't look so sure.

"Why don't you go get yourselves a cup of tea and some cake to eat?" Aveena told them. "I'll ring that bell thing you told me about when I need you."

The look of relief on the women's faces was clear as they scurried away, closely followed by the boy.

Aveena turned to the Riders, her eyes twinkling mischievously. Krystal couldn't help herself and started laughing. The others soon joined in.

It will be a while before this one is tamed, Krystal thought. *But that's good. She's got spirit.*

"Well, I think you're going to be fine here," Willow said.

Aveena's eyes went wide. "You can't leave me yet," she said. "Will you stay? Just for a while?"

"I think that can be arranged," Krystal said.

The Unicorn Riders stayed at Roark for another

week, making sure Aveena was happy and settled in her new surroundings and her new role. Before returning home, they oversaw the transportation of Duke Bowral under heavy guard to a remote retreat in the Nayveen Mountains. Ever since his enchantment by Estrella, the duke had been a different man. He had given up all desire to become king and had promised never again to cause trouble.

"I truly believe Duke Bowral has changed for the good," General Savina said. "But we'll be keeping a close eye on him anyway."

When the Riders finally trotted into their compound in Keydell, Jala ran out to greet them. "Well done on the successful completion of such an important mission," she said. "Queen Heart is thrilled with you all. As usual."

"It's mostly thanks to Krystal," Quinn said. "She's the one who persevered with Aveena every step of the way."

Willow and Ellabeth agreed.

"I couldn't have done it without your help," Krystal said to her friends.

"And to show her gratitude for your latest success, Queen Heart is holding a banquet in your honor tonight," Jala said, beaming proudly. "You've got one hour to get ready and then it's off to the palace."

"One hour?" Ellabeth asked. "That's not nearly enough time."

"What are you talking about, Ellabeth?" Krystal said. "You never spend more than one minute getting ready."

"I don't mean me," Ellabeth said. "I mean you. You're going to need way more than an hour to get ready."

"How come?" Krystal asked.

"Well, your luxurious golden hair seems to have grown back again," Ellabeth said, giggling.

Shocked, Krystal grasped hold of her hair. She pulled it around in front of her so she could see it. "Oh, my goodness!" Krystal exclaimed. It has grown back. Can you see that?"

Jala and the other girls laughed.

"Don't worry, we see it," Quinn said.

"And it's looking more luxurious and golden than ever before," Ellabeth teased. "If that's possible."

"How did it happen?" Krystal asked.

"Must be fairy magic," Willow said.

Yes, Krystal thought with a smile. *That must be it. Fairy magic.*

As she followed the others inside, Krystal whispered a secret thank you to the sky.

Glossary

camouflage (KA-muh-flahzh)—coloring or covering that makes animals, people, and objects look like their surroundings

depleted (di-PLEET-id)—emptied or used up

determination (di-tur-muh-NAY-shuhn)—a strong will to do something

elusive (ee-LOO-siv)—clever at hiding or being able to escape

heir (AIR)—someone who has been or will be left a title, property, or money

marquee (mar-KEE)—a large tent set up for an outdoor event, such as a party

persevere (pur-suh-VEER)—to continue to do or try to do something, even if you have difficulties or are unlikely to succeed

reclusive (RECK-loose-ive)—living a life away from others

reluctant (ri-LUHK-tuhnt)—hesitant or unwilling to do something

sacrifice (SAK-ruh-fise)—to give up something important or enjoyable for a good reason

tedious (TEE-dee-uhs)—tiring and boring

totem (TOH-tuhm)—a plant, animal, or other natural object that represents a person

Discussion Questions

1. What were some of the reasons Aveena didn't want to go back to Haartsfeld?

2. In what ways was Krystal able to relate to Aveena?

3. Why do you think it was hard for Krystal to cut off her hair? Do you think she did the right thing?

Writing Prompts

1. If you could be a queen or a Unicorn Rider, would you? Why or why not?

2. If you could pick a totem for yourself, what would it be and why?

3. What do you think would have happened to Haartsfeld if Duke Bowral had become King?

UNICORN RIDERS

Ellabeth's Test

Krystal's Choice

Quinn's Riddles

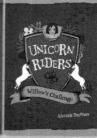

Willow's Challenge

Quinn's Truth

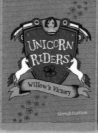

Willow's Victory

Ellabeth's Light

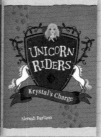

Krystal's Charge

COLLECT THE SERIES!